Little, Brown and Company

Hachette Book Group
1290 Avenue of the Americas, New York, NY 10104
Visit us at lb-kids.com

Little, Brown and Company is a division of Hachette Book Group, Inc.
The Little, Brown name and logo are trademarks of Hachette Book Group, Inc.

The publisher is not responsible for websites (or their content) that are not owned by the publisher.

First Edition: July 2016

Library of Congress Control Number: 2016935672

ISBN 978-0-316-36144-6

10 9 8 7 6 5 4 3 2 1

RRD-C

Printed in the United States of America

KUBO
AND THE TWO STRINGS

THE JUNIOR NOVEL

By SADIE CHESTERFIELD

Screenplay by
MARC HAIMES
CHRIS BUTLER

Story by
SHANNON TINDLE
MARC HAIMES

Ⓛ Ⓑ

Little, Brown and Company
New York Boston

PROLOGUE

The moon was full that night, so many years before. The sea was merciless. Wave after wave rose and fell, some fifty feet tall. Far off, the wind howled. Its urgent voice was joined only by the sound of the sea and a simple, beautiful melody.

A Japanese woman with thick jet-black hair sat on the bow of a small fishing boat. In her hands she held a *shamisen*. The shamisen had been part of Japan's culture for centuries. The instrument had three strings and a long neck, and it was played with a wide pick—a *bachi*. The woman brought the bachi down across its strings, striking a sweet, soulful chord.

As she played, a massive wave came toward the vessel. She stood up, letting the rain strike her face. The wave must have been fifty or sixty feet tall. It came closer, threatening to crush the small wooden boat.

The woman raised her hand, then brought the bachi down across the strings. A clear, pure note filled the air. Ahead of her, the giant wave parted, letting the boat pass through to calmer waters.

She could see the shore ahead now. The journey was almost over, and she was relieved, thinking of dry land. She clutched the straps of the woven bag she'd carried for hundreds of miles. The cloth had a small black beetle embroidered onto it. As the boat neared the beach, she smiled, relieved to be close.

She was so happy that she didn't feel the water pulling back beneath the boat. She didn't see the next wave, bigger than the one before, coming toward the beach. Before she could look over her shoulder, it was upon her, tossing her from the bow. She plunged into the cold, clear water, twisting in the ocean's undercurrents.

The wild sea raged beneath the boat. She tumbled over and over again toward the shore, finally landing on the rocky beach. Her head struck something hard. For a moment everything was black. When she finally opened her eyes, her hair was tangled in front of her face, covering a fresh wound.

Somewhere down the beach, she heard a familiar sound. A baby's cry. She spotted the woven bag a few yards away. It took all her strength to crawl toward it, inch by inch. When she unfolded the thick cloth, she saw that the baby was scared but unharmed. The bandage was still wrapped tightly around his head, covering his missing left eye.

"Kubo," she whispered softly, hugging her son to her heart.

CHAPTER
One

The village streets were packed. A small crowd gathered around a puppeteer, watching as he dangled marionettes over giggling children. Artisans sold carved lanterns. The fishmongers had carted in their latest catch: beautiful red shrimp crawling over heaps of shimmering fish. An old woman bartered for the finest silk kimono.

It was the second day of the Obon Festival. The annual festival had been celebrated in Japan for more than five hundred years as a way to honor one's ancestors. Families returned to their ancestors' graves to clean them, and the ancestors' spirits would visit to consult on household affairs. The three-day festival was a time of love and celebration.

Beside the main road, beggars and street performers held out small bamboo bowls, hoping for coins. Two old men played *shogi*, a Japanese board game, with a few friends looking on. As the village bustled with activity, a voice cried out over the noise.

"If you must blink, do it now!"

The crowd fell silent. A twelve-year-old boy had appeared in the middle of the square. A black patch covered his missing left eye. He held his shamisen in one hand, and his other was raised in the air, clutching his bachi. He brought it down over the strings, filling the square with sweet music.

"Pay careful attention to everything you see and hear," the boy said as the crowd circled him. "No matter how unusual it may seem!"

Whispers spread through the streets. They'd seen the boy—Kubo—perform before, but each time he was more hypnotizing. He paced around, looking into his audience's eyes. "And please be warned. If you fidget, if you look away, if you forget any part of what I tell you, even for an instant"— he pointed to a random woman in the crowd, speaking slowly and dramatically—"then our hero will surely perish!"

Kubo leaned back, strumming his shamisen with his eye closed. He was playing a happy tune when suddenly something red burst out of the woven bag on his back. It flew through the air in a blur, somersaulting the length of the crowd before landing right in front of him.

The origami warrior stood just six inches tall. He was a simple man, made of cherry-red paper. Kubo held up his hand to silence everyone. "Hanzo was a mighty samurai," he started. "But he was alone; his family had been taken from him, his kingdom in ruins, and his army destroyed by the dreaded Moon King. You may recall, Hanzo was roaming the distant Far Lands in search of a magical suit of armor: the only weapon in the whole world that could protect him from the power of the Moon King. This armor was made up of three pieces. The first..."

Kubo scanned the crowd, waiting for an answer.

Akihiro pushed through. "Oh, oh, oh! I know!

The Sword Unbreakable!"

Kubo lifted his hand and plucked the first string on the shamisen. A piece of cherry-red paper flew out of his bag and folded in midair, forming the famous sword. Hanzo grabbed it and swung it around his head while the crowd cheered.

Kubo ran to the other side of the circle, kneeling down beside a little girl named Mari. "The second?"

"The Breastplate Im..." Mari tried to sound out the word. "Im-pen-uh-truh-ble!"

Kubo struck the second string on the shamisen and another piece of paper came out of his bag, magically folding into a breastplate. It sat on little Hanzo's chest, protecting his heart.

"And, finally, the third weapon," Kubo said. "The final piece of the armor..."

His friend, Kameyo, a local beggar woman, sat at the edge of the circle. Her tattered blue kimono was patched in places, and her white hair was pulled into a bun. She raised her hand.

"I know this one! The Helmet Invulnerable!" she shouted.

Kubo plucked the third string, and another piece

of cherry-red paper shot out of his bag, folding into Hanzo's helmet. It fit perfectly on his tiny head. The crowd clapped and cheered. A little boy in the front row kept pointing at the tiny warrior and squealing in delight.

Kubo went on, pacing around the audience, playing notes on the shamisen. "But before Hanzo could claim the armor and unite the pieces to reveal their true power, he was attacked by the Moon King's beasts...."

He played a dark, moody chord, and the crowd fell silent again. He spun around, and a black piece of paper flew into the air, reforming into a giant spider. It crept toward the hero. Hanzo raised his sword, slashing at its legs.

The show continued. A ferocious shark swallowed Hanzo whole, so the hero had to fight his way out from the inside, turning the shark into confetti. A fire-breathing chicken belched flames at Hanzo. He ran toward it, coming just inches from the fire, when he folded back into a flat piece of paper. He slid below the chicken, reforming on the other side of him.

Furious, the chicken shot paper eggs at Hanzo.

Hanzo sprang into action. He took a few steps and leaped into the air, somersaulting over the chicken with his sword outstretched. In one swift motion, he chopped off the chicken's head. A man in the front of the crowd covered his daughter's eyes, not wanting her to see.

Kubo kept the show going all day, telling stories of his hero, Hanzo. He struck another chord on his shamisen.

"Hanzo was filled with rage," he said, "his soul tormented by the grief of a family stolen from him."

Kubo played a slower, more ominous tune, and a blue piece of paper rose from his pack. It folded into a dark, terrifying silhouette.

"At last, our hero was face-to-face with his nemesis, the Moon King!"

The two figures flew into the air, ready for battle. Kubo raised his bachi, ready to play another tune, when the sound of the town bell interrupted him. The clangs rang high above the village, signaling the setting sun. Kubo lowered his hand, and the figures unfolded, the sheets of colorful paper slipping back into his bag.

"Be sure to come back tomorrow!" he called out as he gathered up a few coins people had left for him.

The crowd groaned. One annoyed woman shook her fist in the air.

"What?"Akihiro, said. "Oh, come on! People like an ending, please? Where are you going? No...you can't leave!"

But Kubo did just that, hurrying through the packed square and down the road, not stopping until he was home.

CHAPTER
Two

Kubo walked up the steep path just as the bell finished chiming, approaching a cave nestled on top of a jagged cliff overlooking the sea. His mother was sitting where he'd left her that morning, at the back of it, staring out at the setting sun. He sat down next to her, resting his hand on her arm.

"Kubo," she whispered, suddenly realizing he was there.

"Yes, Mother, I'm here," he said. "Hungry?"

She nodded, so he went to work on dinner. He lit

the fire and set rice and fish in a pot to cook. They ate slowly, and often Kubo had to catch the rice that had fallen down her chin. She'd been sick for years now. Sometimes she would be clear and calm and know exactly who he was. But other times she would have trouble talking or even eating, and she would forget where she was and who was with her. Kubo used the money he made in the square each day for their clothes and food.

When they finished dinner, he assembled his origami samurai warrior and his monkey charm beside him. He'd had the charm ever since he could remember. Standing only three inches high, it was supposed to be a good luck charm for protection. The three sat around the fire, listening as his mother told a story.

"Even though he could barely see his own hand in front of his face, Hanzo and his army of loyal samurai pressed on through the blizzard." His mother was her best self tonight, now energized by their meal. She pretended to step through deep snow. "And suddenly, as quickly as it had started, the storm cleared before him. Hanzo breathed a sigh of relief, for he was home."

Kubo straightened up. "His fortress? The Beetle Clan castle?"

"Yes," his mother said. "At the very edge of The Far Lands. Hidden from the Moon King by powerful magic…"

"And then what happened?" Kubo asked. "When he got to the castle?"

His mother took a long pause. She stared at her feet, losing her train of thought. "When who got to the castle?"

"Hanzo, my father," he reminded her.

"Hanzo was at the castle?" She rubbed her head, trying to remember what she'd said. "Just give me a second…I'm sorry, Kubo. I can't. Perhaps I could recall a different story?"

Kubo smiled, taking his mother's hand. He tried to make her feel comfortable and safe whenever she couldn't remember. She was sick—he knew she was—and it was getting worse each day. Sometimes at dawn she could barely speak. Sometimes she couldn't even remember his name. He worried what would happen when things got worse, and there was only him to take care of her. Would he be able to?

"Why don't you tell me what father was like?" Kubo asked.

"Oh, this one is easy." His mother laughed, beginning her tale again. "Hanzo was a mighty warrior, skilled with sword and bow."

"No," Kubo said. "What was he *really* like? When he wasn't fighting. When he was with us?"

She leaned down and looked into Kubo's eye. "He was just like you. Strong and clever and funny. And oh-so-handsome." She pinched his cheek playfully.

"Ugh! Mother!" Kubo giggled.

But then she got quiet, her face suddenly serious. "Never forget how much he loved you, Kubo. He died protecting us."

"Did the Moon King—"

"Your grandfather," his mother corrected.

"Did Grandfather and your sisters really kill my father? It can't be true, can it? They're family."

His mother's eyes widened. She grabbed his shoulders, bringing him close to her. "They're *monsters.* Grandfather and my sisters stole your eye, Kubo. They must never find you again, ever. You must always stay hidden from the night sky, or they will find you and take you away from me. Promise me you'll never let this happen."

Kubo's eye filled with tears. It was in these moments that he felt the most alone. How could he promise his mother that? How did he know what the future held for either of them, or what would happen? He would try, of course he would try, to hide from them....But could he hide forever?

His mother must've noticed the fear in his eye, because she let go of him. She glanced down, picking up the tiny monkey charm. "Don't be sad, Kubo," she said, making the monkey speak in a silly voice. "Remember what you must do?"

"Keep you with me at all times," Kubo said, nodding.

"And...?" his mother asked.

"And keep my father's robe on my back at all times."

"Yes, Kubo," she said, resting a hand on his shoulder. The red robe was a little big for him, but he would grow into it. "And there's one more thing. Never, ever, stay out after dark."

Kubo nodded, knowing that this was the most important thing his mother had ever told him. If he was out after dark, the Moon King would be able to see him far below and come for his other eye. It was why he ran home every night when the village bell rang. It was why they hid, alone in this cave, night after night.

"Remember?" his mother repeated, pretending the monkey was speaking to him.

"Yes, Mr. Monkey," Kubo said, letting out a small laugh.

Then they laughed together. They huddled beside the fire, keeping warm before bedtime.

CHAPTER
Three

The next morning, the streets were alive again. Women in a line did an elaborate dance, sweeping their arms up into the air and spinning around as a crowd watched. Colorful lanterns decorated the buildings on the square. As Kubo walked through the festival, he spotted his good friend Kameyo sitting on a nearby curb.

"Paper Boy!" She smiled, revealing her missing front teeth. "Come sit next to me. I got us a good spot here."

Kubo sat beside his friend, and together they watched the women spin and dance, the music swelling around them. "I do so love the festival," Kameyo said. "A time to celebrate. You know, it's a shame you never stay past sundown. There are fireworks and singing and dancing and feasting, of course. But the best part of all..."

She pointed to the lanterns that hung outside each doorway. "Do you see those lamps and altars? We use those to speak to the loved ones that left us behind. We listen to their tales and guide their safe return to the blissful pure land."

Kubo had heard this all before, but somehow today it felt different. Was he old enough now, wise enough, to contact his father? If he lit a lantern in his honor, maybe he'd come back for him.

"Really?" Kubo asked in surprise. "Did you speak to someone?"

"Yes, I did. My husband. His voice was as clear and loud as the one you use for your stories. In seventy-two years he never had a thing to say. Now that he's gone, I can't shut him up!"

Kubo couldn't help but smile.

"You have someone you'd like to talk to, huh?" Kameyo said, noticing his expression. "Well, what's stopping you?"

"Do I need a lamp?" Kubo asked, looking at the ornate altars that lined the square.

"I bet you could make a really nice one with that paper-folding thing you do." She gave him a friendly nudge, pointing to the cemetery. "Now hurry along, go! There's still time before dark!"

Kubo stood, taking off through the square just as the dance ended. He turned back one last time, waving good-bye to his friend.

Kubo kept walking, finally seeing a break in the forest ahead. The road opened up into a beautiful, lush cemetery, the sun low in the sky above it. Flowers bloomed. Tree branches twisted above him. On the grassy hills, dozens of families knelt with their unlit lanterns, waiting for their loved ones to visit.

He found a clearing and dropped his bag and

supplies. Using a big rock as an altar, he set to work on his lantern. He folded the ivory paper several times, creating an elaborate lantern with windows in its sides. He watched a family nearby, listening to the conversation to try to figure out what to do next. Asking the dead to visit didn't come naturally to him.

A man, Hosato, was just a few yards away. He directed his daughter to place the lamp on the altar. As the little girl did that, Kubo set his lantern on his altar, too. Then Hosato told his daughter to pray to their loved one, a grandmother. Kubo wasn't quite sure what to say to his father, but he began anyway.

"Hello, Father," he said. "I hope you're well. Uh...I mean, I know you're dead, but I hope everything is...okay."

Kubo cringed, thinking of the spirit of his father somewhere listening to him bungle the prayer. He could do better. He'd start over—pretend as if it never even happened. Maybe his father hadn't heard....

"Look, it's your robe!" he said brightly, holding up the cloth covering his shoulders. "Mother says I'll grow into it. She says you were a great leader who died protecting me. Saving one of my eyes. Two would've been ideal, but...thanks anyway."

Kubo let out a small laugh, hoping his dad got the joke. He waited, listening to the wind, but he couldn't hear anything. He wondered if his dad even knew he was there.

"Father..." he went on. "I'm worried about Mother. With every day that goes by, she drifts further away. She talks a lot about you, but...I just don't know. I don't think she remembers what's real anymore. *I* don't know what's real anymore...."

Kubo took a deep breath, tears welling in his eye. "I just wish you were here. So I could talk to you, see you...find out what I should do."

He was about to say more, but a small voice interrupted him. "Daddy! Daddy! Grandma is here!"

He turned and saw the family beside him peering into their lamp. The wick had burst magically into flames, lighting the lantern. Hosato smiled as he and his daughter walked down to the river, setting their lantern on the water to help their grandmother return to the spirit world. The little girl chatted happily to her grandmother as they went.

Kubo stared into his lantern. It was still dark, the

wick just the same as when he had made it. Why hadn't his father come? Where was he? Had he listened to even a word Kubo had said?

"Father? *Hellooooooo?*" Kubo called, staring into the orange sky. The sun was starting to fall behind the mountains. He would have to return to the cave soon.

Kubo folded his arms across his chest. "Any time..."

But still, his father didn't come. He watched the families in the cemetery smile and laugh as their lanterns lit. A young couple clutched each other as they walked their lantern down to the river and watched it float out to sea. Kubo sat in front of his altar, wishing the lantern would light, but minutes passed and nothing happened.

Soon he was alone in the cemetery. He looked to the sky, waiting again for a sign, but there was nothing.

"Fine!" he said, snatching the lantern off the altar. "I don't need you anyway!"

He crumpled the paper lantern and threw it into the grass. He'd never felt so alone. Why had all the other spirits visited but not his father's? Why wasn't his prayer answered?

He sat down in the grass, staring at the balled-up paper. He picked it up and smoothed it out, not noticing the sound in the distance: the village bell marking the sunset. He looked down at the broken lantern in his hands. "I'm...I'm sorry...."

He wasn't sure to whom he was talking, but he felt better apologizing for his foolishness. He had been wrong to get so angry with his father. If he hadn't visited, Kubo would return next year to find him, and then he would say something different—the right thing that would make him come back.

The wind whipped through the cemetery. Kubo turned, suddenly noticing how dark it had become. The hills were silent. The sky had turned a deep blue.

All along the river, the lit lanterns were extinguished one by one. Wisps of smoke curled from their charred wicks, joined by a thick fog rolling in off the bank. Through the trees, he swore he heard something: a strange, melodic voice whispering his name.

He spun around, trying to see where the voice

was coming from. It was calling to him. His heart was thumping fast in his chest, and he immediately started to worry. What had he done? How had he not noticed how late it had gotten?

Then he saw her. There, across the river, was a woman dressed in long, billowing robes made of crow feathers. Her hair was the color of squid ink, just like his mother's. Her wide-brimmed hat was pulled down, the front of it so low he could not see her face. She held a long wooden pipe in one hand.

"Little boy," she said, coming toward him, "what happened to your eye?"

Kubo took a step backward, but she only came closer, laughing a horrible, high-pitched laugh. He heard more laughter and another woman stepped out from the first woman's shadow. She looked the same as the first one, with the same black hair and wide-brimmed hat. They both had a silver medallion covering their hearts.

"Who are you?" Kubo called out. He tried to sound brave, but his voice was shaky. "How do you know my name?"

"We're your family, Kubo," the women said. "Your mother's sisters. And we've been looking for you for so long. It's so lovely to meet you... face-to-face."

As they said it, they both raised their chins, showing themselves to him. But their faces were hidden behind ghostly white masks. Their lips were fixed in permanent smiles, and their black eyes stared at him blankly. Kubo had seen the *Noh* masks before—they were part of Japanese culture—but he'd never seen ones as terrifying as these. All the hairs on the back of his neck stood up.

"Come, Kubo, come to your aunties...."

As they glided over the river toward him, he watched in horror, too scared to even move. "No reason to be afraid, Kubo...." they said. "We just need your other eye. Your grandfather admires it so...."

They started up the bank toward him. He turned, running in the opposite direction, back toward the village. He glanced over his shoulder and saw one of the sisters take a puff on her wooden pipe. Smoke blew out of the pipe and curled up above her, taking on a terrifying shape. Smoke demons filled the sky, descending upon him, ready to strike.

"Help!" he screamed, running as fast as he could. "Somebody, help! Look out! Run!"

CHAPTER
Four

Kubo didn't stop running until he got to the edge of the village. He held tight to the gates, trying to catch his breath. Behind him, the demons were still coming for him, a fog of twisting, curling smoke.

"Run!" Kubo shouted as loud as he could. "Quick!"

But his voice was so small compared with the fireworks that exploded in the sky above him. The crowd in the square was so thick that no one could hear him over the shouts and cheers. Women sang and danced, the music so loud it drowned out all other sounds.

Kubo ran into the market, trying to warn the villagers. But just as he did, the terrible black smoke split in several directions, spreading out over the large crowd. It coated the village like a fog, setting buildings ablaze and sending people running for cover.

He ran with a group of scared villagers who turned away, ducking inside one of the buildings that were still standing. Kubo kept on, thinking only of his mother in the cave. She must've felt so alone and scared. She waited every sunset for him to come home. She must've known what was happening out here in the night.

The terrible smoke slithered over the town. Kubo sprinted as fast as he could, finally reaching the path that led to the cave. But in an instant the smoke was upon him, too. Then his aunts appeared, emerging from the darkness.

"We're here, Kubo," they said, coming up the path toward him. "Your family has come for you."

He tried to run but he tripped, falling forward onto the path. The smoke was everywhere. Terrified, he laid his head down on the ground. They would take his eye, he was sure of it, and maybe his life, too.

Then he felt a tug on his woven bag. The sweet chords of his shamisen filled the air. He looked up, worried that the Sisters had taken his beloved instrument, but it was his mother standing before him. She brought the bachi down across the strings, strumming a beautiful tune.

The notes were so powerful that they moved through the smoke like a shock wave, stunning the demons. For a moment, the smoke fell back. Kubo stood quickly, starting toward his mother as she played. She never took her eyes off her evil sisters.

"Kubo, you must find the armor," she gasped. "It's your only chance—remember this!"

He wanted to hug her, to hold her close, but there was no time. She shoved the shamisen into his arms. Then she held her hand out. It glowed with a mysterious blue light. She gently touched the beetle that was embroidered on the back of his father's robe. Within seconds magical wings sprouted from the folds of the cloth. They fluttered furiously and Kubo was slowly lifted into the air.

Up, higher and higher, he went, until his mother

was so small below him. He watched helplessly as his aunts moved toward her. One drew a razor-sharp sword. The other pulled a bladed chain from her robes. His mother was surrounded.

He watched, terrified, as his aunts moved in. They charged his mother with great force, but just as they reached her there was a blinding light. Then the robe rose up around him, shielding his eyes.

CHAPTER
Five

When Kubo awoke, his hands were throbbing. His head was buried in snow, and every part of him was freezing. Somewhere, he could hear a woman calling his name.

"Kubo? Can you hear me, Kubo?" she cried. Kubo turned, staring up at the woman…who wasn't a woman at all. A monkey stood next to him. She was four feet tall, with a pink face and thick white fur. She stared down at him with narrow brown eyes.

Kubo jumped up, struggling to get away from the creature. But everywhere he turned, there was nothing but white. They were in the middle of a blizzard, the snow coming at them sideways. He could barely hear what she was saying over the sound of the wind.

The monkey stepped forward. "I said your mother is gone. Your village is destroyed. Burned to the ground. We landed here in The Far Lands, but your enemies aren't far behind. We must search for shelter before your grandfather comes."

Kubo stumbled backward, unsure what to do. He tripped over his bag and nearly crushed his shamisen. Then, below his feet, he heard a low creaking sound. He wasn't in a field of snow—he was on a sheet of ice. The monkey spun around, gesturing for him to get on her back.

"We need to go now," she said. "Come on!"

He turned around, looking at the frozen lake. There was snow in every direction. Where was he supposed to go? What was he supposed to do? He'd never even been outside his village before. Now he was here, in The Far Lands, somewhere he had heard about only in stories.

He climbed on, hoping that she would take him to safety.

The monkey moved easily over the snowy terrain. With her help, Kubo could go twice as fast as he would have on his own. She carried him all day, showing no signs of tiring, and it wasn't until they reached the edge of a glacier that she stopped to rest.

Kubo glanced at the sky, suddenly realizing hours had passed since he awoke. The monkey stepped forward, gesturing to something beyond the glacier. Part of it was covered with snow, but Kubo could make out just enough to recognize the body of a dead whale.

"Once we're inside," the monkey said, "you might be tempted to complain about the odor. Keep in mind—my sense of smell is ten times stronger than yours." As the sun started to set, the monkey ducked inside the whale's mouth, waving for Kubo to follow.

The stench was disgusting. Kubo tried to hold his breath as the monkey went to work, tending to a small fire beneath the whale's blowhole. She cooked some sort of soup in a large conch shell, stirring it with a piece of bone.

"You have questions," she finally said. "I can tell. You get three."

"Why only three?" Kubo asked.

"Okay, that was your first question," the monkey said.

"What?" Kubo snapped. "I don't understand what's happening. Who are you?"

The monkey looked up, staring into his eye. Then she sat down and quickly posed exactly like his monkey charm. "You don't recognize me....All these years you had to keep me in your pack. Now you know why."

"But you were a wooden charm!" Kubo cried, confused. "You were so small. I called that charm *Mr.* Monkey!"

"If I were alive at that point, I might've found

that insulting," the monkey said tersely. "Look, your mother used the last of her magic to save you and bring me to life."

Kubo stared at the ground, thinking of what she said. *The last of her magic. Your mother is gone. Your village is destroyed.*

They'd been moving all day, and everything had felt scary and new. It was only now, in the quiet of the night, that Kubo began to feel the sadness of what had happened.

"Here, drink," the monkey said, handing him a clamshell filled with white liquid.

"It smells," Kubo mumbled. "I don't want it."

"I said, drink it," the monkey repeated, an edge to her voice.

"You're a mean monkey, aren't you?" Kubo shot back.

"Yes, I am," she said, holding up a few fingers. "And that's three. You're out of questions now, so just listen. I'm here to protect you, Kubo, and that means you have to do as I say. So if you don't eat, you'll be weak. If you're weak, you'll be slow. If you're slow, you'll die."

Kubo took the soup, bringing the clamshell to his lips. He slurped away, making a loud, annoying show of it. "Oh, excuse me," he said, pretending he did it by accident.

"You better start taking this seriously, Kubo!" the monkey said, pacing the length of the whale. "This is real. This is not a story. Those things, your aunts, they *never* get hungry. They *never* sleep. They *will* find you, and if we're not prepared...they'll kill me and take your other eye."

Kubo swallowed the liquid, quiet for a moment. "So...what are we going to do?"

"We're going to find the armor!" the monkey said. "It's the only thing that can protect you."

"So it's real. It's really real...."

The monkey nodded. Kubo looked down, trying to imagine what it would be like to find the armor in real life.

That's when he spotted the strand of thick black hair on his robe. He plucked it off, examining it in the firelight.

The monkey reached out for the strand of hair, but Kubo backed away.

"Don't worry," she said. "I'm not going to keep it."

"I must've pulled it from her head," Kubo said, remembering reaching for her before the robe lifted him into the air. "I didn't mean to."

The monkey pinched the hair between her knees, then braided the length of it, tying the end in a knot. "Your mother was very powerful. She blessed your robes so that when the need was most, they would fly you away. She used the last of that power to bring me to life. This bracelet, her hair; it's a memory. Memories are powerful things, Kubo. Never lose it."

She tied the bracelet around Kubo's wrist. Kubo stared at it, the hair he'd know anywhere, its straight, thick strands so much like his own. It was comforting to have a bit of his mother still with him.

Maybe the monkey was right—maybe it would help him.

"One more question?" Kubo asked.

"Last one," the monkey said.

"Do you know where it is? The armor?"

The monkey poked at the fire with a whalebone, letting the sparks fly through the air. "No," she said.

"No, I don't. Now go to sleep...."

Kubo wrapped his robe around him like a blanket. When he buried his face in it, it smelled a little like home—a mixture of the beach and the smoke from their fires. He breathed in, trying to tell himself that Monkey would protect him. She was there to keep him safe. But as he lay down to sleep, he kept thinking of the Sisters, with their cold, blank stares, descending on his mother before she died.

CHAPTER
Six

The next morning, Monkey was standing over him, looking confused. "You were talking in your sleep," she said. "Calling out to your father. And then the paper flew out of your bag and folded itself into... him."

She pointed to the other side of the whale, where Little Hanzo was standing, his sword raised in the air. He was bigger than the Little Hanzo that performed in Kubo's shows, and looked as if he'd been made out of several pieces of red paper. He had a beetle on his breastplate and textured armor. Kubo walked over to him, trying to figure out what had happened.

"He's been standing there for hours," Monkey said. "Quietly judging us. I'm not even sure this counts as origami. I could swear scissors were involved."

Kubo leaned over, reaching out his hand, but the tiny warrior knocked it away with his paper sword. "Back home in the cave, it was my mother's dreams that did this. And the paper always unfolded itself by morning."

The two watched as Little Hanzo climbed on top of Kubo's bag, striking a regal pose. His sword pointed at the whale's blowhole. Kubo leaned over and turned the bag in another direction, so Little Hanzo's sword was pointing the other way. Little Hanzo turned and pointed to the blowhole again, as if he was trying to tell them something really important.

"What are you doing?" Kubo asked.

Little Hanzo pointed at Kubo, then at the blow-hole, as if to say *Come on, let's go already!* Kubo turned back to Monkey and shrugged. "I guess this is how my father answered me."

Monkey let out a deep breath. "I'm tempted to say that trusting our fate to the guidance of a small paper man seems like a bad idea. But...it's the best bad idea we have."

Little Hanzo climbed out of the blowhole, and Kubo and Monkey followed closely behind. Outside, the sun was already bright in the sky. Little Hanzo led the way, pointing his sword toward an area beyond the glacier. Then he jumped on Kubo's shamisen for a ride.

They walked to the far side of the glacier, then down through the foothills. The land was covered with a thick layer of snow. Kubo heard chirping above him and looked up, noticing a small white bird in the sky. He plucked a few strings on his shamisen, and a piece of ivory paper flew out of his bag and folded into a bird, joining the real one.

Monkey heard Kubo laughing and turned around, wanting him to hurry along. But he looked so happy watching the birds. For the very first time since they were together, he seemed at peace, almost carefree. He strummed his shamisen, and several more sheets of paper flew up and folded into birds, creating a whole flock.

Kubo's birds flew, flipping and turning at his command. They glittered in the sunlight, somersaulting in a dazzling dance of paper wings.

"You're getting stronger," Monkey said.

Kubo let out a deep laugh. He could feel his magic growing. Was it his mother? Or his father's spirit helping him, as he had asked?

"You might not want to look quite so pleased about it," Monkey went on. "We grow stronger. The world grows more dangerous. Life has a way of keeping things balanced."

Kubo curled his lip, sneering. "Monkey, do you ever say anything encouraging?"

"I encourage you not to die," Monkey said, smoothing down Kubo's robe. Then she took off in the direction Little Hanzo had shown them.

Kubo followed, struck by a silly idea. He sent one of his paper birds flying down from the sky. It swooped right behind Monkey, nipping her butt. She spun around, but the bird had already disappeared into the flock.

Kubo stared at her innocently. "Mosquitoes," he said, swatting at his neck. "Annoying."

Monkey turned back around, walking through the thick snow. Then, without orders from Kubo, the whole flock flew down behind her. They re-formed into three giant mosquitoes. For a moment Kubo thought Monkey hadn't noticed. But then she reached out, snatching the first mosquito in her hand. She kicked behind her, knocking out the second mosquito, then somersaulted backward to destroy the third one.

When she was done, she returned the sheets of paper to Kubo's bag.

"Paper runs out," she snapped at him. "As does patience."

"I didn't ask them to do that...." Kubo started. "...The second time. At least, not exactly. I mean, I felt it, but—"

"Magic is not meant to be easy," Monkey said. "You need to learn control. Concentrate on what you're doing. And always remember"—she leaned in close, her pink nose right in front of him—"don't mess with the monkey."

She turned, continuing through the snow. They walked like that for hours, with Monkey lecturing Kubo on everything from magic to origami. Monkey told him that he should be more careful where he stepped, that he needed to eat more so he could grow up to be tall and strong. She wanted him to get better at his sword skills and learn more chords on the shamisen. Kubo listened to it all, barely saying a word. It was starting to feel as if he couldn't do anything right.

They came to a stretch of land with a massive statue half-buried in the snow. There was a giant head, covered with an ornate helmet, sticking out from underneath the drifts.

Monkey turned back, pointing at the broken hand ahead, its stone fingers clutching a broken sword.

"Tread carefully, Kubo," she said. "This isn't one of your stories."

Kubo rolled his eye. He slowed down, letting her get farther ahead of him. When Monkey was a few yards off, he climbed up a nearby statue, sitting for a moment on its face. There was a giant hole where one of its eyes should've been. If he had peered inside, he could see the hole went all the way down, forming a long tunnel.

"How do you know?" Kubo shouted at her back. He stood, putting his hands on his hips. "Maybe it is. And I'm the valiant hero. And you're the mean monkey."

"You may think you're the great hero," Monkey said, not bothering to turn around. "But heroes come and go. Any moment, something terrible could come out of nowhere and—"

"Monkey!" Kubo yelled, his voice filled with terror.

Monkey spun around, but Kubo was nowhere to be seen. She ran up the giant stone face just in time to see Kubo several yards down the tunnel. He was being carried by some giant creature with two sets of arms. They kept going, farther down the pit, until they finally disappeared into the dark.

Monkey grabbed the edge of the statue, curled into a tight ball, and slid down after him.

CHAPTER
Seven

Monkey flew through the tunnel. It twisted and turned, winding down into the center of the earth. As she got deeper inside the huge cavern, the walls were carved with the faces of ancient gods long since forgotten. When the tunnel finally leveled out, she could see Kubo ahead of her. He was still being carried by the strange creature.

She ran as fast as she could, following the kidnapper through a maze of tunnels. The walls of the cavern were filthy and crumbling. She kept after them, turning when they turned and treading down a steep incline. For a few seconds she lost sight of them, but then there was a sharp turn. The tunnel dead-ended in a large cave.

The creature was right in front of her now. It was three times her size, with a thick black shell like a beetle's, which was scarred and chipped in places. Horns came out of either side of its head. It had two sets of arms and could run on the ground like a bug. Its face was human, though, like that of a samurai warrior. She narrowed her eyes, then charged the beast with great fury.

"Monkey, wait!" Kubo cried. He stepped out of the darkness, holding his hands up in front of the beetle, trying to stop her. "He wasn't trying to hurt me. He just wanted Hanzo."

The beetle leaned over, staring at the little paper warrior. "Hanzo?" he asked. "Hanzo..."

Monkey's eyes were still wide. It felt as if her heart were beating a million times a minute. "I still think I'm going to stab him...." she mumbled.

The beetle reached out one spiky claw, gently stroking the tiny Hanzo. "Hanzo...yes," he said. "I remember him. I think maybe…he was my master."

"What?" Kubo asked. "What did you just say?"

Then the beetle stood up straight, looking at Monkey and Kubo as if he'd only just realized they were there. He kept shaking his head.

"We had a crest," he said. "A samurai crest!" He spun around, digging through a pile in the corner of the cave. There was a bow and arrows and some samurai swords. He pulled out a huge piece of red fabric with the familiar beetle crest on it. "Have you seen this crest before?"

Kubo turned, showing the beetle the back of his robe. It was the same exact image. Beetle's eyes lit up with excitement. "It's a miracle! You have our robe! You're wearing our robe!" Then he stopped suddenly. He narrowed his eyes, suspicious. "*Why* are you wearing our robe?"

Before Kubo could respond, Monkey stepped forward. "He doesn't have to answer your questions. Anyway, who are *you*?"

"Many years ago I was cursed," Beetle said. "Trapped in this cursed state. Cursed to wander The Far Lands. No comrades. No master. Not even a name or a single memory of the noble warrior I once was."

"You used to be a man?" Kubo asked.

"Not just any man. A samurai," Beetle said. "I mean...I'm pretty certain. I have the stuff." He gestured at the pile behind him. Every sword and piece of armor had the beetle crest on it. "I mean, I'm either a samurai or a really bad hoarder. Either way, inside my thorax beats the heart of a warrior."

Monkey narrowed her eyes at Beetle, not sure she could believe him. "If you still have no memory, how can you be certain of anything?"

"Because I get flashes. They come about from objects I find on my travels. Or sometimes it's a sound. Or a smell." Beetle suddenly looked sad. "But the memories—they fade, and all I'm left with is this sense that I was once part of something much greater."

Kubo stared at the giant creature's face, feeling a tug of sympathy for him. He seemed so alone...and so scared. Kubo turned back to Monkey. "Can I tell him?"

Monkey held up her hands. "I really don't think that's a good idea...."

"Hanzo was my father," Kubo blurted out.

"Kubo!" Monkey shouted.

But Beetle only smiled. "This is a miracle! I have found the son of my master."

Beetle scooped Kubo up into a hug, then danced around the cave with him, humming happily to himself. When he finally set him down, he dropped to his knee. "Whatever brings you to these lands, whatever your quest, it is now my quest, too. I will join you. I will give my life for you if necessary!"

"Wow..." Kubo said, looking into Beetle's eyes. "You will?"

Beetle nodded. "Do you think that's possible? I mean, I know how quests go. People die all the time. They drop like flies. But that doesn't matter, because I have a feeling this is my destiny!"

"No, it isn't!" Monkey stomped her foot in anger. "We can't trust anything you say, because *you* can't trust anything you say. We don't know anything about you."

Kubo plucked a few notes on his shamisen and a piece of paper flew from his bag. It folded into a bird and hovered right between Monkey and Beetle, breaking the tension. "Monkey, you said it yourself," Kubo started. "Our quest is a difficult one. A samurai—even a cursed one with no memory who looks like a bug—could be helpful."

"Yes, I'm certain I could be helpful!" Beetle cried, looking excited. "Indispensable!"

"In what way?" Monkey put her hands on her hips.

Beetle grabbed his bow and arrow. He set the arrow in its place, then pulled back the bow, letting it fly into the wall. It landed perfectly straight.

Monkey just laughed. "Firing an arrow into a wall is hardly what I'd call—"

Beetle shot another arrow at the first one, splitting it down the middle. Then he fired three more, one after the other, splitting the second with the third, then the third with the fourth, then the fourth with the fifth. All of them were perfect bull's-eyes.

Beetle dropped down, kneeling in front of Kubo once more. "Just tell me of our quest," he said. "And

I will immediately demonstrate my numerous indispensabilities."

"Well, that's kind of a long story," Kubo said.

"You've got my attention. I promise I won't even blink." Then Beetle turned his head, making his eyes as wide as he could. "I actually don't even think I can blink. Do I have eyelids?"

Monkey let out a deep breath, finally accepting their new friend. "Fine—walk and talk," she said, nodding toward Little Hanzo. He was standing at the far end of the cave, his sword pointed down a dark tunnel. "Hanzo has found a path."

"So you used to be a *toy* monkey?" Beetle said, turning to Monkey in disbelief.

"Kubo, I really don't see how this part is important to the story...." Monkey said, trying to interrupt. Kubo had been telling Beetle about his small town, and what it was like living in the cave by the sea.

"Yes!" Kubo cried. "I used to keep her in my pocket. She was so tiny. And I called her *Mr.* Monkey."

"I wasn't a *toy*," Monkey said, clearly annoyed. "I was a *charm*."

Beetle laughed a big, hearty laugh. "Of course you were...."

Suddenly, Little Hanzo leaped from Kubo's shoulder and ran down the tunnel. He flattened himself into a single piece of paper, then slipped through a mossy crack in the wall. Beetle broke through the wall to follow him, and all of a sudden they were face-to-face with a giant carved statue. The skull had huge, hollow eyes and a terrible sneer. Kubo got chills just looking at it.

It was a dead end—there was nowhere else to go. But Little Hanzo kept pointing at the statues ahead of them. Kubo stepped forward, peering at the stone, trying to see if he was missing anything. Where did Hanzo want them to go? What were they missing?

"Don't touch anything!" Monkey yelled.

But Beetle was already running his claws over the statue. He touched one of the skull's front teeth, tugging at it to see if the stone was solid. The tooth came off in his hands. There was a loud, horrible *click*!

Beetle and Kubo turned to Monkey, their faces pale.

"He did it," Beetle said, pointing to Kubo.

But before Monkey could respond, the floor gave out beneath them. They all plummeted hundreds of feet into a dark cavern below.

CHAPTER
Eight

Oof! All the air left Kubo's lungs. For a second he just lay on the ground, trying to catch his breath. Beside him, Beetle rocked back and forth on his shell, unable to get up.

"Kubo, look!" Monkey said. She'd already sprung to her feet and was standing in the center of the cave. Giant bones were scattered all over the floor. In the center of them was a skeleton's hand, its palm open. Inside the palm was a beautiful silver sword.

"The Sword Unbreakable!" Kubo cried. He stood up, rushing toward the sword. Monkey grabbed him and held him back.

"It could be a trap," she said.

Beetle scuttled forward. "Allow me."

"What, it's not a trap if you do it?" Monkey asked.

"*Stealth* is my middle name," Beetle replied. He reached across the bony palm and grabbed the end of the sword. Then he spun around, showing it to Kubo. The silver sparkled in the light.

"Ha-ha!" Beetle laughed. "The mighty Beetle is victorious!"

Almost as soon as he said it, the fingers of the hand started to move. The floor of the cave trembled. Then, one by one, the scattered bones rose into the air. Monkey and Kubo darted around, trying not to get hit by them.

Beetle ran back to his friends in terror.

They looked up, two fiery eyes staring at them. A giant skull came down from the roof of the cave as the bones came up to meet it. Slowly, it formed a giant skeleton three stories high, covered with terrible armor made of broken bones.

The giant skeleton came to life, stomping toward them. Monkey knew she had to act fast. Beetle stood frozen, just staring at it.

"Oh, for crying out loud," she said, grabbing the sword from Beetle's claws. She held it up in front of her. "I invoke the Sword Unbreakable!"

Monkey leaped into the air, bringing the sword down across the giant skeleton's leg. The blade shattered into a hundred pieces. She stood there, staring at the handle, which was still intact. "It broke."

"So does it just mean the handle, or...?" Beetle asked. "I'm a little disappointed in this magic sword."

"It's not the right sword, you idiot!" Monkey yelled.

Just then, Little Hanzo popped his head out of Kubo's bag. He pointed his paper sword at the skeleton's head. All at once, they noticed the skeleton's crown. It was made of dozens of metal swords sticking out of its skull.

"The sword! It's in his head!" Beetle yelled. Then he turned to the skeleton. "Hey...I've got a bone to pick with you!"

He pulled the bow and arrow from his back and fired. Then he fired a dozen more, trying to kill the skeleton, but most of the arrows just bounced off his bones. A few more flew straight through the gaps between his ribs.

"Uh…this is problematic," Beetle mumbled.

Unfazed, the skeleton reached down and scooped up Monkey in its hand. Beetle unleashed a volley of arrows, but they all bounced off. Some flew right past Monkey's head.

"Enough with the arrows!" she shouted, ducking as one nearly took off her ear.

As the skeleton lifted Monkey higher, she got closer to its skull. She reached through its horrible, bony fingers and grabbed one of the swords, smashing it against the monster's hand. The sword shattered into a hundred pieces.

She tried another sword, then another, but they all shattered when she slashed at the monster's bones. Angry, it dangled Monkey over its giant mouth, about to chomp off her head.

Then a familiar melody echoed through the cave.

As Kubo played his shamisen, hundreds of pieces of paper flew from his bag and folded into birds. They swarmed the skeleton's skull in a giant flock. The monster shrieked and cried as they swiped at him, hitting him in the head.

As the monster swatted at the paper birds, it kept lifting its giant bony feet into the air, then stomping them back down again. Kubo and Beetle ran across the cave floor, trying to avoid them, but it was no use. Kubo couldn't run fast enough. The monster's foot was just seconds away from crushing him.

Beetle jumped forward, trying to push him out of the way. For a moment it seemed hopeless. The giant foot was right over their heads, about to smash them both. Then, suddenly...they were flying.

They zipped around the cave. Beetle held Kubo tightly, and they both glanced over their shoulders, looking back at the jet-black wings that had shot out of Beetle's shell.

"You can *fly*?" Kubo asked.

"Apparently, yes!" Beetle cried. He rocketed them into the air, toward the beast's skull. They crash-landed right on top of the monster's head, Monkey in its hand beside them.

They didn't waste time. They pulled the swords from the skull, trying to find the right one.

Beetle pulled one out and smashed it against the skeleton's head. It shattered into a hundred pieces. "Are you sure it isn't called the Sword Unfindable?" he asked, grabbing another handle.

Kubo tried three in a row, but all broke apart. Then he noticed Beetle struggling to pull a sword free from the skull. "A little hand here?" Beetle asked.

Before Kubo could step forward, the monster reached for Beetle, his bony hand like a cage. The skeleton yelled and roared, lifting Monkey and Beetle into the air, about to chomp them into bits. Kubo reached for the sword but was thrown high into the air when the monster moved.

Then he was falling, the ground coming fast to meet him, until an arrow shot straight through his robe. He hung by the cloth, pinned to the cave's ceiling.

Beetle had saved him with his perfect shot. Kubo

Kubo lives in a small village, where he earns a simple living by putting on shows for the town's marketplace. He's a very popular storyteller.

One reason he's so well liked is his magical origami— he brings elaborately folded pieces of paper to life, telling tales of legendary samurai and evil kings.

But one night, the evil Moon King finds Kubo after years of fruitless searching. He sends his daughters, two shadowy sisters with blank masks hiding their faces, to collect Kubo and destroy his village.

Kubo is forced to flee, but he's not alone. He has a protector—a talking monkey who used to be a simple charm Kubo's mother gave him. And along the way...

...they meet Beetle, a large, talented warrior who doesn't remember who he was or what his purpose is.

The only way to stop the Moon King is to assemble the three legendary pieces of armor—the Sword Unbreakable, the Breastplate Impenetrable, and the Helmet Invulnerable.

But each piece has a fierce guardian...

The two Sisters are hot on Kubo's trail, even following him to the middle of a huge lake.

And while Monkey fights to keep them away from Kubo, the boy is locked in a battle of his own with the second guardian.

Even through all of his trials, Kubo is determined to stop the Moon King.

But the road is long, and continuing on means facing even more danger, and eventually the Moon King himself.

The three companions must work together if they are to have any hope of succeeding.

The Moon King fiercely pursues Kubo. He will use all of his great power to take him away to live forever in the sky.

watched from above as the monster skulked around the cave. He was totally helpless.

Then the robe ripped a tiny bit, and a tiny bit more. He was going to fall; he knew it. Monkey briefly escaped the skeleton's hand, trying to save Kubo, but within seconds the monster grabbed her again.

Kubo cringed as he heard the final, horrible rip of the cloth. He fell fast toward the ground. But just at the last second, the giant skeleton bent forward, accidentally giving Kubo the perfect landing spot.

As soon as Kubo touched down on the monster's skull, he went to work, pulling at the many swords in the skeleton's crown. He smashed several on the beast's skull until he found the same handle Beetle had discovered. He took a deep breath, then pulled it as hard as he could, yanking it free.

Beetle and Monkey looked up at Kubo, who stood with the sword raised above his head. He was smiling, so relieved to finally have it in his hands.

"Thank goodness that's over," Beetle said.

But within seconds the skeleton started falling

apart, bone by bone. It was as if the Sword Unbreakable were the very thing that held it together. Kubo looked at the skull beneath his feet, which was turning now, no longer held up by the monster's neck. He closed his eyes as they all fell fast toward the earth.

CHAPTER
Nine

Kubo played his shamisen as he walked along the rocky beach. The music almost drowned out the sounds of Monkey and Beetle arguing....

Almost.

"Look, I appreciate your help, but when it comes to the boy, I really know what's best," Monkey said. "And what's best is to not be fielding ideas from a talking cockroach."

"This coming from the talking monkey," Beetle said.

At first, they argued about how to cross Long Lake, which spread out in front of them. Then they debated how powerful Kubo's magic was, and now Beetle told Monkey she was too protective. They were so silly when they fought, making jokes back and forth, that they started reminding Kubo of the fishmonger and his wife from his village.

Kubo kept playing his shamisen, trying to ignore them. After they'd fallen from the giant bone monster, Beetle used his wings to fly them to safety. They flew through the maze of tunnels, then out onto the rocky shores of Long Lake, which Monkey knew from folklore and cave paintings. Monkey had used some mud to help repair Beetle's wings, but after his crash landing on the beach, they were too broken to fly very well.

The beach was covered with fallen leaves of yellow, orange, and gold. Giant pieces of driftwood had washed ashore long ago. As Monkey and Beetle argued about crossing the lake, Kubo played on. One by one the leaves and driftwood lifted from the shore, coming together to form a ship that was shaped like an origami boat. Monkey turned around, shocked by how impressive it was. With that, Kubo plucked a final note, creating a sail made up of grass and leaves.

They climbed aboard and set off. Beetle and Kubo used arrows to fish, and soon they were all eating sashimi. Little Hanzo speared a piece of fish and flipped it into Beetle's mouth.

"Must you play with your food?" Monkey asked.

"Yes." Beetle smiled. He turned to Kubo, expecting a laugh, but Kubo had a strange look on his face. "What's the matter, Kubo? You act like you've never had a meal sitting between a monkey and a beetle before."

"I've never had a meal sitting between *anyone* before," Kubo said. He couldn't help but feel a little happy here, with Beetle and Monkey, two creatures who cared enough to fight over him. He had loved being with his mother in the cave, but it had been lonely sometimes.

"Kubo, question," Beetle said. "Before you started your heroic quest, what were you like?"

"Well, I looked after my mother mostly," Kubo said after a long pause. "Sometimes I would tell her stories about little things, like catching fireflies in the mulberry fields. And when I told those stories, I could tell her eyes were mostly clear. I could tell she saw me, really saw me. And I saw her, too—her spirit, trying to find its way out."

Beetle glanced sideways at Monkey and smiled. "You know what, Kubo? Before you went on this great adventure, you were still very much a hero."

Kubo could feel his cheeks turn red. He was about to thank Beetle for saying such a nice thing, but then thunder echoed in the distance. They looked at the sky, which had turned a dark gray. A storm was coming.

"We're going to have to head for shore," Monkey said. "Find a hiding place."

They watched as Little Hanzo marched up to the bow of the ship. He pulled out his sword, and they waited for him to show them the best direction to sail. But when he lowered it, he was aiming at the dark waters below them. Kubo leaned over to see what he was trying to tell them.

"The second piece of armor!" he said, noticing the shiny metal breastplate under the water.

"I got it!" Beetle cried. He grabbed the side of the

ship and started to hop over.

"Beetle, wait!" Kubo said. "My mother told me a story about Long Lake. She said there was a Garden of Eyes under the water. Eyes that stare into you. They show you secrets, things to keep you down there with them forever."

Beetle looked into the water uncertainly. "Well, I won't look directly into anyone's eyes. Even if I'm being incredibly sincere."

Then he was gone, disappearing into the waves with a *splash*!

The rain was coming down hard now. The waves tossed the ship this way and that. Kubo kept peering into the dark water below, but there was no sign of Beetle. He knew beetles could hold their breaths for a long time....But *how* long? Shouldn't he have come back by now?

"Monkey, I think he's in trouble," Kubo said. "We should help him."

Monkey nervously paced the length of the ship. "Kubo, your aunts are still out there," she said, looking at the gray storm clouds above. They'd waited long enough for Beetle. She was sad to leave, but they had to—it looked as if it was already past sunset. "We should head for shore."

Monkey heard a *splash!* somewhere behind her. When she turned back around, she realized Kubo was gone. She peered over the side of the boat, but she couldn't see him beneath the waves. She grabbed the Sword Unbreakable and headed to the bow, trying to find the best spot to go in. He was somewhere below....But where?

She dove off the bow. Before she hit the water, she was yanked back. She twisted and turned, but someone was holding on to her ankle.

She spun around, trying to free herself, but then she saw the Sister's horrible face. The Sister was wearing the same terrible mask, her lips fixed in a sneer.

"Look at this...." the Sister said, still clutching Monkey's ankle. "I come fishing, and all I reel in is this stinking ape. How pathetic that *this* filthy creature is all that's left of my sister's magic."

Monkey gritted her teeth. She used all her strength to break free, springing onto the deck of the ship. She held the Sword Unbreakable out in front of her, prepared to fight.

"This filthy creature will tear you apart!" she yelled, then charged toward her.

CHAPTER
Ten

Lightning and thunder tore apart the sky. Monkey darted around the boat, trying to avoid the savage blows from the Sister's razor-sharp chain. They'd been fighting for what felt like forever, and the Sword Unbreakable had been thrown across the deck. It was perched high above her, just out of reach.

As Monkey dodged all the Sister's blows, the deck started to come apart beneath her feet. It was Kubo's magic that had created the boat and held it together. She knew that he must be in trouble somewhere below the water, that he was close to death. How long had he been under the surface? How could she save him now, with the Sister after her?

The Sister saw Monkey's worry and used it to her advantage. Her chain flew out and coiled around Monkey, trapping her. "I have crushed creatures who have fit this whole world on their fingernail," she said. "This victory brings me no honor."

As the Sister moved to strike, Monkey kicked free. "Imagine how you're going to feel when you lose," she said, flipping over her to the top of the bow. She landed right beside the Sword Unbreakable.

"I felt loss only once," the Sister said, as Monkey launched her own attack. She dodged Monkey's blows. "Eleven years ago, I lost my sister. She fell in love with a fool and betrayed our father. She was an ungrateful coward!"

Monkey was closing in, about to strike, when the Sister disappeared into the clouds and rain. All Monkey heard were her strange giggles echoing in the air around her.

"Who's the coward now?" Monkey asked.

No one responded. Before Monkey could say

anything else, Little Hanzo pointed to the ship's sail, which was unfurled behind them. Monkey spun around in confusion. Sister wasn't there.

Then, in an instant, the sail fell to the ship's deck. Sister was hiding behind it, ready to attack from behind. She struck Monkey with the chain. Monkey fell, her head smashing against the deck.

As the Sister stepped forward, Beetle appeared at the side of the boat. He held a fish, skewered with an arrow, in his hand. Monkey frowned, knowing that Beetle must've gone beneath the water, then completely forgotten why he was there.

"I got it!" Beetle cried.

"Where's Kubo?" Monkey called out. "Get back down there! He's in trouble!"

Beetle's face changed from happy to terrified as he slowly realized that he had forgotten about Kubo. He hopped back over the ship's side, disappearing into the water as the Sister stalked forward. She struck Monkey again. The Sword Unbreakable flew from Monkey's hands, landing in the side of the wooden ship.

Monkey flipped to the other side of the ship,

landing a quick blow to the Sister's ribs. They fought on, Monkey dodging the horrible chain again and again. Soon the ship was just a few large pieces of driftwood, which Monkey jumped back and forth between, trying to stay safe.

"It never fails to amaze me how the creatures down here fight so hard just to die another day," the Sister sneered.

"Down here, there are days worth fighting for," Monkey shot back.

"There is nothing down here worth anything!" the Sister yelled.

Monkey spotted the Sword Unbreakable on a long, broken piece of the ship. She ran toward it, but before she could grab the handle, the Sister's chain coiled around her. She fell, still trying to reach it.

"It's pathetic what happened to my sister," the Sister said. "I looked up to her. She was so strong. Love made her weak."

Monkey turned, staring up at the Sister and remembering who she was. It all came back to her in that moment—their father, the Moon King, and the life she led before she met Hanzo. She'd tried to push

it out of her thoughts for so long, but this sister—
they had once been everything to each other. It was
painful to see what strangers they had become.

"No," Monkey said, narrowing her eyes. "It made
me *stronger.*"

Then she leaped forward, grabbing the sword and
spinning around. She closed in on her sister with a
new power. This had to end—now. When she finally
raised the Sword Unbreakable, she knew it would be
for the last time.

Far below the waves, Kubo swam toward the
breastplate. He could see the metal glinting through
the seaweed as he weaved between schools of colorful
fish. As soon as he reached it, he slipped inside the
Breastplate Impenetrable, the suit magically shrink-
ing to fit him. But when he turned to swim back, he
noticed a strange glow coming from the deep.

The sea monster was staring at him with its one
horrible eye. It was the creature his mother had

warned him about, a giant underwater beast with thousands of legs. Kubo didn't want to look at it, but he couldn't help himself, and soon he was staring back. His limbs went limp. He could no longer think. All he wanted was to go with the monster deeper into the dark.

Whispers chattered in the gloom below. The giant eye took Kubo with him, down into the bottom of the lake, and Kubo was powerless to break free. He stared into the eye, hardly noticing a far bigger monster beneath them, one with a giant mouth lined with razor-sharp teeth. There were thousands of eyes below, all staring up at them, bringing him deeper into the trance.

Then something flew past his head with a *whish*! An arrow punctured the glowing eye, and the underwater monster let out a painful shriek, the sound rippling through the water. Another arrow flew past Kubo's head, and he turned to see Beetle swimming toward him, his bow aimed at the giant monster below.

One by one, Beetle shot arrows into the glowing eyes as the monsters twisted in pain. Kubo slowly realized where he was. He'd gone so deep into the lake, and now he'd run out of air, his lungs throbbing. He opened his mouth, and water rushed in.

He tried to call for Beetle, but he couldn't make a sound. His head was spinning. The last thing he saw was Beetle coming toward him. Then everything went dark.

CHAPTER
Eleven

Beetle broke through the surface of the lake, carrying Kubo in his arms. The ship was in ruins. The last pieces of wood floated along the water.

"Over here!" Monkey called out. She clung to what remained of the bow.

Beetle swam to her, pulling Kubo up onto the wreckage. He wasn't moving, and his skin had turned a ghostly gray. "It was the eyes," Beetle said. "They had him in a trance."

"No...." Monkey said, gently shaking Kubo's

limp body. "Wake up! Please wake up. It's going to be all right....I'm here."

Monkey laid her head on Kubo's chest, and the tears streamed down her cheeks. She could hear his heart still beating. But for how long? When would her child come back to her?

When she looked up, she saw the pieces of the boat coming together again. They assembled on the surface of the lake. His magic was still alive...which meant he was still alive. He had to be.

Just then, Kubo started to cough. He turned on his side, the water spewing from his mouth. When he'd finally caught his breath, he looked into Monkey's eyes. "I saw you, *Mother*...."

Monkey stroked his hair, hugging the boy to her chest. "My son," she whispered.

They stayed like that for a long time. Slowly, the boat formed around them. Then they were moving over the water again, the giant sail catching the wind.

Hours later Kubo and Beetle were huddled around a fire. They'd found a cave on the shores of the lake, and they took cover there for the night. Monkey moved around collecting firewood.

Beetle looked from Monkey to Kubo, then back at Monkey. "So you must look more like your dad, then?"

Kubo just shrugged. Monkey hadn't said much while they sailed to shore. He waited for her to explain as they made the fire, and while she speared fish for their dinner, but the whole time she was silent.

"You're staring," Monkey finally said, turning around. "Let me guess. You have questions."

"Tell us your story...please?" Kubo asked.

Monkey seemed unsure. She picked up Kubo's shamisen and handed it to him, a sad smile curling on her lips. "Perhaps you can help me...."

Kubo plucked a few notes, playing for her.

"The night I met your father..." she started, taking a deep breath. "My sisters and I went to the Temple of Bones to kill Hanzo."

Kubo was so stunned he stopped playing, holding his bachi in the air. For a moment the cave was quiet.

"Oh, right..." he mumbled, playing a few more notes so Monkey could start the story. As music filled the air, pebbles and twigs rose up around them, hovering near the ceiling to illustrate what Monkey was saying.

"At the bidding of the Moon King," Monkey went on, "my sisters and I had come down from the night sky and killed many noble warriors. Your grandfather told us that any man who found the magical armor would grow too powerful and be a threat to the heavens. That night, I arrived at the temple before my sisters. And there he was. The mighty Hanzo."

Above them, the twigs and pebbles illustrated the scene—a young Mother and Hanzo together.

"'You have offended my father,' I said, 'Now you must die.'"

"That's so *you*." Beetle laughed.

"We fought," Monkey went on. "Hanzo was strong. But then he stopped. He looked into my eyes and uttered four simple words. These words changed everything."

"I love you, Monkey?" Beetle guessed.

"'You are my quest,' he whispered. I had seen the wonders of the universe, but the warmth of his gaze as I looked into his eyes...*that* I had never known. It was his humanity I saw. And it was more powerful than anything in my cold realm." Monkey watched as the figures danced above them, falling in love. "I spared his life, and he gave me mine."

The figures then appeared with a baby Kubo in their arms. "He gave me you...." Monkey said. "But your grandfather found us. His rage at my betrayal shook the heavens. Your father and his army gave their lives, allowing me to escape with you in my arms."

Kubo stopped playing the shamisen, and the figures slowly fell to the cave floor. "Why does Grandfather hate me?" he asked.

"He doesn't hate you," Monkey said, stroking her hand through Kubo's hair. "He wants to make you just like him. Blind to humanity, as I once was. Only then can you take your place beside him as part of his family."

"I'll never be like him," Kubo said. "Never."

Monkey hugged him, trying to calm his nerves. "I know...."

After a long while, she realized he'd fallen asleep in her arms. She rose, carrying him to the corner of the cave, where she made sure the robe was covering every part of him. Then she returned to the fire.

Beetle watched her limp as she walked. There was blood staining her fur, and she winced when she sat back down. "You're hurt," he said.

"Just a scratch."

He glanced back at Kubo, making sure he was asleep. "Monkey," he started. "Why didn't you tell him sooner who you really are?"

"The magic that keeps me here...it's fading," Monkey said. "Soon I'll be gone, and Kubo will be alone again."

"Not alone," Beetle said. "He is the son of Hanzo, and I will do everything I can to keep him safe from harm."

"Thank you, Beetle. To know Kubo has someone to watch over him when I'm gone...that would be a fine way to end my story."

"Your story will never end," Beetle corrected. Monkey had never seen him so serious. "It will be told by him. And by the people he shares it with. And by the people they share it with. And by the people they share it with. And by the—"

"Beetle!"

"The point is," Beetle said, "your story will live on. In him."

Monkey looked across the cave to where Kubo was sleeping. She listened to each one of his breaths. She didn't know if Beetle was just saying that to be nice, but she wanted to believe him. She smiled, wiping the tears from her eyes.

CHAPTER
Twelve

Kubo sat at the edge of the river. Beside him, a sweet old man was playing a shamisen. A thin white film covered his eyes. Kubo understood that he was blind.

"This is a dream," Kubo said, sensing he was still asleep. "Is it a good one or a bad one?"

"See for yourself," the old man said, gesturing to the fortress in the distance.

Outside it, a row of samurai wore the beetle crest. It must've been Hanzo's fortress. The Helmet Invulnerable floated above the warriors, as if they were guarding it.

"The last piece of armor!" Kubo cried. "It's here?"

"Follow the setting sun, and you'll find it," the man said. "In the place that might've been your home. Claim your birthright, Kubo! Give this story a happy ending!"

In an instant, Kubo woke up. He glanced across the cave at Monkey and Beetle, who were still sound asleep. Immediately, he knew what he must do.

Hours later Kubo, Monkey, and Beetle were on their way to Hanzo's castle. They hiked a trail that cut through the mountains. The sun was just visible behind the clouds, lighting up the sky.

Kubo smiled, knowing they were so close. All they needed to do was get to the fortress, and they would find Hanzo's helmet. They'd been walking for hours....The ruins couldn't be far now.

High above them, a flock of birds glided beneath the clouds. They looked like herons, but their wings glowed with a magical golden light. They sang a song that sounded so much like the one from Kubo's dream. "The Song of the Dead," he remembered one of the villagers calling it.

"Golden heron," Monkey said, pointing at them. "It's believed they hold the souls of the departed, carrying them to wherever they may need to go."

"What are they singing?" Beetle asked.

"Many say the song's about what happens when we die," Monkey explained. "We don't just disappear. Like Kubo's paper, we shift. We transform. So we may continue our story in another place. The ending of one story is the beginning of another."

They stood, watching the beautiful birds. Kubo loved how they dipped and soared, how they separated and came back together again. He hoped Mother was right, that there was no death. He wanted to believe another story was waiting for them.

After a long while, they started walking again, climbing to a high cliff. There, far below, they could see the crumbling castle. The walls and roof were overgrown with wild bamboo.

They took the bridge, finally reaching the main

hall of the fortress. The torn banners that hung on the walls displayed the beetle crest. Weeds climbed the bricks. There were a few broken swords on the floor, but most had been stolen long ago by vandals.

"I remember this place," Beetle said, glancing around.

Kubo found a room off the main hall. The screen guarding it had a picture of his parents when Kubo was just a baby. Broken furniture was strewn about. The floorboards were rotted, with weeds sprouting through.

There was a desk with pictures of the Underwater Garden of Eyes and the Hall of Bones Skeleton, and scrolls and maps pinned to the walls. "This must be where my father prepared for his quest," Kubo said. At the far end of the room, he noticed screens with pictures of the helmet on them. Behind the screens was a wide courtyard.

Kubo pushed inside. The sky was visible above, the moon peeking over the edge of the building. Rusted samurai armor was scattered across the bricks. Kubo looked around, searching for the helmet, but it wasn't there.

"There's something I don't understand...." Beetle said. "Why would the helmet be here?"

Almost as soon as he said it, dark smoke descended on the courtyard. Thin tendrils snaked around them, lifting Monkey, Beetle, and Kubo high into the air, as the sound of laughter rose up around them. Beetle's bow fell from his grasp, clattering to the ground.

The last Sister came down from the darkened sky. She floated into the courtyard, watching Monkey, a terrible sneer on her face. "Oh, sister," she said, "I remember how we looked up to you. Of all of us, you shone the brightest. Such a waste. All we wished was to be a family...in our home among the stars."

"I think we have very different definitions of family," Monkey shot back.

The Sister reached out to touch Kubo, as Beetle fought to free himself from the smoke. "Don't touch him, you witch!" Beetle yelled.

The Sister turned to Beetle, staring at him with cold, blank eyes. "Then there's you," she said. "The thieving insect who stole my sister's soul."

Beetle and Monkey looked at each other, unsure what she meant. The Sister let out another horrible laugh. "Oh, this is precious!" she said. "You've been together all this time and you haven't realized? You took her from us. It was only fitting that we took something from you. How swiftly those memories spilled from your head. Wiping out all recollection of your obscene union, Hanzo."

She brought her pipe to her lips, and a dark puff of the smoke came from the pipe and circled Little Hanzo, raising the origami figure into the air. The figure unfolded itself, the paper turning flat again, then reforming into a perfect replica of Beetle.

Beetle shook his head, unable to believe it. The Sisters had stolen his memory. This whole time, when he was down in those dark tunnels, it was because of them and their spite. He hadn't even recognized his own son.

"I didn't know," Beetle said, looking at Kubo with tears in his eyes.

The Sister just laughed. She tossed Beetle into the wall, his body making a hollow sound as he fell. Then she stalked forward, toward Kubo.

"I'm forgetting what I came here for," she said.

The smoke twisted around Kubo, holding him tightly. He was just able to reach his hand around the back of his belt. As the Sister came close, he slashed at her face with his bachi. Her pipe hit the ground and shattered. Her ceramic mask cracked in half, revealing her mouth. Within seconds all the smoke demons disappeared, their source gone.

The Sister screamed in Kubo's face, then threw him across the courtyard. Monkey came at her from the other side, wielding the Sword Unbreakable. The Sister pulled two crescent blades from her robes, and they started to fight, the weapons crashing and clanking against each other as they moved through the courtyard.

Monkey darted past the Sister, dodging her blows. She struck the sword against the small blades again and again. But she was tired from the night before, and the wound in her side throbbed. Slowly, her sister was gaining the upper hand. As the Sister floated above Monkey, preparing to deliver the final blow, a rusted metal sword hit her in her side.

Across the courtyard, Beetle was now awake. He

threw every piece of armor he could find at her, trying to stop the attack. The Sister staggered and fell. For a moment everything was quiet.

Beetle ran to Monkey, who'd crawled across the courtyard to Kubo. Kubo held her in his arms, noticing the deep wound in her side. She was bleeding. *"Shhhh*…it's okay," Kubo said, trying to comfort her. "I'm here."

"My son," Beetle said. He rested his claw on Kubo's shoulder.

"Seems I'm married to a bug," Monkey said weakly.

"A samurai bug." Beetle laughed. Then he looked down at her, smiling. "You are my quest. You always have been."

"Hanzo…" Monkey said, taking her last breaths. "Keep him safe. No matter what."

"I promise I will." Beetle was about to go on, but the Sister appeared behind him, plunging her blade deep into his back.

"No!" Kubo cried, watching as his father fell.

The Sister moved in, raising the blades again, this time over Monkey's head.

"Fly home, Kubo," his mother said, pushing him away.

Kubo ran across the courtyard. He found his shamisen underneath his armor. He held the bachi high in the air as the Sister's blades came down on his mother's neck. He played the notes so hard two strings snapped in half. Then the sound of the shamisen filled the courtyard. Everything was bathed in a blinding white light.

CHAPTER
Thirteen

Kubo wasn't sure how much time had passed. When he woke up, the courtyard was empty. The Sister's broken mask was on the ground a few feet away. Then he spotted Beetle's broken bow. It was sitting next to the monkey charm, which had cracked into two pieces.

Kubo knelt there, his shamisen in his hands, two of its strings broken and frayed. Tears fell from his eye onto the remaining string, sounding a sad, sorrowful note. Behind him, the paper rose up and folded itself. Little Hanzo was still with him. He looked tattered and dirty, but he was there.

The tiny paper warrior crawled forward, pointing his sword at something on the far wall. Kubo finally turned, noticing a drawing of the Helmet Invulnerable. He tilted his head to the side, seeing what Little Hanzo was looking at. From such a long angle, the Helmet Invulnerable looked exactly like one of the bells in the village bell tower.

Kubo kept staring at it, realizing what this meant. The last piece of armor was still waiting for him. He could still defeat the Moon King as long as he was brave enough to go find it.

He packed up his bag, putting Little Hanzo and the monkey charm inside. Then he picked up Beetle's bow. He pulled off the bow string, and wrapped it around his wrist, making a bracelet like the one he had of his mother's hair. He stood in the middle of the courtyard with his shamisen in his hands.

The tattered banners that hung on the walls flapped in the wind. Kubo lifted his bachi. Then he looked at the sky and played the last note, striking the shamisen so hard the final string snapped in two.

The banners flew up into the air, breaking free from their mounts. Then they folded and reformed above him, turning into a beautiful pair of wings. They joined the back of his robe and lifted him high above the crumbling fortress. He watched as it grew so small below him, finally disappearing against the mountains.

Kubo's new wings flew him high above the village. From there, he could see the charred ruins of the stores and cafes and the crater that had once been the square where he'd performed. He landed just steps from the broken bell tower. It was still standing, the last bricks looking dangerously close to crumbling.

Kubo stared at the burnt scaffolding that surrounded the bell. There was so little time—the Moon King was coming for him soon. He pushed the weakened structure, then slashed at it with the Sword Unbreakable. Within minutes it came tumbling down, the Helmet Invulnerable glinting in the wreckage.

He picked it up and dusted it off. Then he heard a small voice from somewhere behind him. "Kubo, is that you?"

He turned to see his friend Kameyo. Her face was covered with soot. She peered at him from the doorway of a ruined house. Behind her he saw Hosato and Mari, two of the other villagers he'd known so well.

"You have to leave this place," Kubo called out. "The Moon King, he is coming."

He watched as the villagers hurried off, never feeling more alone in his life. When he was sure they were safe, he put the Helmet Invulnerable on and turned to the sky. "Grandfather! It's me, Kubo!" he yelled. "I know you can see me!"

For a moment the village was silent. Kubo felt the hairs on the back of his neck stand up, as though he was suddenly in danger. He spun around to see the blind old man from his dream. Only now the man was wearing elegant robes that glowed in the moonlight. He stared at him, his eyes white with cataracts.

"Hello, Grandson," the man said. "You have found the armor. Seems your mother had a reason to bring you to this dreadful place after all."

Terrified, Kubo snatched a rock from the ground and threw it at the old man. But the man's hand shot up, catching it in his palm. "I see," he said.

"I know you do," Kubo said. "That's how this all began. You finally saw me. That was my fault. I should have listened to my mother."

"Kubo," the old man said as he strode forward. "We both want the exact same thing."

"You want my other eye, that's what you want," Kubo shot back.

"As long as you cling to that silly, useless eye, you can't come live with me in the heavens." The old man stepped closer. "You'll be stuck down here in this hell. Staring with that lonely eye at hate and heartache and suffering and death. Where I want to take you, we have none of those things. It will just be you with your family."

"My family is gone," Kubo said, staring at him. "You killed them."

"They brought their fates upon themselves," his grandfather said. "They disgraced me and upset the order of everything."

"That's how your story goes."

"Oh, Kubo," his grandfather said. "When you're up there with me, you will be beyond stories. You will be immortal. You will be...infinite."

"No, you're wrong," Kubo snapped. "Not infinite. All stories have an end...and this story ends when I kill you."

He held the Sword Unbreakable in front of him, watching as the Moon King's skin began to change. It took on a ghostly white glow, then became more wrinkled and hard-looking, as though it were a terrible shell.

"Oh, very well," his grandfather replied. "Is this what you want? To do battle with the hideous monster who ruined your life? To prove your worth like your doomed father? How mortal."

At that, his grandfather threw open his arms, and his body cracked in half. From it emerged a giant white monster, several stories tall, with hideous fangs and a long, spiky tail. It looked like something between a shark and a snake, slithering through the air. Kubo held up the Sword Unbreakable and ran at it, trying to land the first blow.

The beast stalked forward, snapping at him. Kubo flipped over its side, dragging the Sword Unbreakable along the beast's body. But when the Sword Unbreakable touched it, it sparked as if the monster's skin were made of metal. Still, the beast stumbled back, surprised by the attack.

Kubo stepped forward, swinging the Sword Unbreakable again and again, which pushed the monster farther back. As soon as Kubo had the advantage, he lunged at it, jabbing the Sword Unbreakable into the monster's eye. It swung its tail around, knocking over a charred building behind it.

The giant beast was furious. It charged Kubo, but he was too quick. He spun around, jumping through a nearby window, and darted out the other side of the building. The beast kept after him, chasing him through the narrow streets of the village. Kubo ducked and weaved to avoid the monster's blows, occasionally landing the Sword Unbreakable in its side. He ran as fast as he could, but as he approached the edge of the village, he struggled to catch his breath.

Exhausted, Kubo tripped over some rubble in the street. As soon as he fell, the beast was upon him. Its jaws locked down around his body. The armor buckled under the pressure, and Kubo fell from beneath the Breastplate Impenetrable, where he crashed through a broken wall. Slowly, he stood in front of the monster, bruised and bloody, his heart exposed.

The creature snapped its tail like a whip, the end curling around Kubo. The spiky end flipped the Helmet Invulnerable off his head. Big globs of spit flew at Kubo's face as it bellowed. "You want to be human? Then share their weakness!"

The tail coiled tighter, squeezing Kubo to death. He gasped for air, his face turning blood red.

"Suffer their humiliation!" the beast went on. Its spiky tail ripped Kubo's eye patch off his face. "Feel their pain!"

The beast slammed Kubo onto the ground. Kubo could see the Sword Unbreakable just a few feet away.

He crawled toward it, knowing it was his last chance, but it was already too late. With a flick of its tail, the monster grabbed Kubo and sent Kubo careening into the cemetery.

CHAPTER
Fourteen

Kubo crashed through trees and bushes, tumbling down the cemetery hillside. His bag broke, its contents scattered in the grass. He could barely move. Every part of his body hurt. But he could hear the monster crashing through the forest, coming for him with frightening speed.

Kubo slowly pulled himself off the ground. He looked at the Sword Unbreakable lying a few feet away, then at the shamisen, all its strings now broken. He reached out for the Sword Unbreakable, suddenly noticing the two bracelets on his wrist. One made from his mother's hair, the other from Beetle's bow.

He pulled the shamisen into his lap. As fast as he could, he began restringing the instrument. The beast was coming closer. As he tied the last end of his bracelet onto the shamisen, he heard it at the edge of the cemetery, looking for him. There were still only two strings, though—where would he find the last one to complete the instrument?

The monster rushed inside the cemetery gates, finding Kubo immediately. It looked down on him, teeth bared. "This is the end of your story," it growled. "Now take one last look with that lonely eye. One last look at this wretched place you call home."

Kubo stood, defiant. He reached up and plucked a hair from his head, stretching it across the shamisen. "I'm not leaving," he shot back. "For every horrible thing down here, there's something far more beautiful. My mother saw it. So did my father. I see it, even with just one eye."

"Then I'll just have to rip it out of your head again, won't I?" the beast growled.

The Moon Beast stalked forward, but before he

could strike, Kubo strummed the shamisen. A booming note split the air.

"If you must blink, do it now!" Kubo cried.

All the lanterns in the river suddenly sparked to life. They lit the river, showing its snaking route out to sea. The cemetery was filled with light.

"I know why you want my eye," Kubo said. "Because without it, I can't look into the eyes of another and see their soul. Their love."

"Everything you loved is gone," the beast yelled. "Everything you knew has been taken from you."

"No," Kubo said. "It's in my memories. The most powerful kind of magic there is."

Kubo plucked the second string. From behind the trees appeared the surviving villagers. They each held a lantern as they took their place beside Kubo. Then Kubo plucked the final string. More figures came out from the forest, but they glowed with the same beautiful golden light the herons did. They were the spirits of the villagers who had long since passed.

"It makes us stronger than you'll ever be," Kubo said, gesturing to his new army. "These are the memories of those we have loved and lost. And if we hold their stories deep in our hearts, then you will never take them away from us."

Kubo stood and looked up at the terrifying beast, daring it to strike. The Moon Beast wheeled back and lunged like a snake. But as the fanged head neared the army, it was deflected by a glowing blue light. The monster pulled back, stunned, then moved to strike again. Each time it was blocked by the light, which glowed even brighter than before.

"And that really is the least of it," Kubo added. With that, he brought his hand down on the shamisen, strumming all three notes. The blue light exploded across the cemetery. Then, suddenly, everything was a beautiful white.

CHAPTER
Fifteen

The light was so bright Kubo couldn't see anything. When it finally faded, the cemetery was calm. The giant beast was gone. Standing in front of him was the gentle old man from his dream. He smiled kindly.

"Where am I?" he asked.

Sensing that something powerful had happened, Kubo walked toward him. He knelt in front of him. "Hello, Grandfather," he said.

The man looked confused. "I'm sorry, young

man, but I seem to have forgotten my story. Can you help me?"

The people in the crowd looked at one another, realizing what had happened. The powerful magic that had brought the spirits to Earth had taken the Moon King's memory, turning him into an ordinary old man. The love they felt for one another had made him human again. Kameyo stepped forward, seeing an opportunity.

"I'll tell him. No—we'll all tell him. We'll tell him everything he needs to know," she said. Then she turned to the old man. "You are the kindest, sweetest man to ever live in this village."

"Really?" the old man said.

Mari stepped forward. "Every day you walk around smiling and handing out coins to children like me."

"*And* old women!" Kameyo added.

One by one, more villagers stepped forward.

"You taught my kids to swim!" the fishmonger called out.

"You fed the hungry," an elderly woman said.

"You're a good man," Akihiro added.

"A great example," the owner of the kimono shop said.

Kameyo leaned in close and pointed to Kubo. "You know, we have something in common. We both adore your grandson. His name is Kubo."

The old man rubbed his forehead and frowned. "Kubo, I'm sorry…" he said softly, "but I don't remember."

"Well, your grandson's a storyteller," Kameyo said. "He'll tell you all the stories you've forgotten."

"Really?" the old man said.

Kubo looked at his grandfather, who was so different from the man who stood before him just hours before. His face didn't have the same harsh lines. He was frail and kind, and he smiled when he spoke. Maybe Kubo wasn't alone after all….Maybe he'd have his grandfather from now on.

"Of course I'll tell you," Kubo said, taking his hand.

EPILOGUE

Later that night, all the villagers walked down to the river, accompanied by their loved ones' spirits. Each villager held a glowing lantern in their hands. As they got to the river's edge, they set the lanterns in the water, watching the current pull them away. They each said their last good-byes to their loved ones, then they turned and headed back to the village.

Kubo made another altar on the riverbank. He put two new paper lanterns on top of it, then knelt down. "Hello, Mother; hello, Father," he said. "I know my stories can tend to get a little, um, long...so

I'll keep this brief. I am very grateful I had the chance to meet you both. Hear your wisdom. Feel your kindness. Even eat a meal sitting between you. This was a happy story...but it could still be a whole lot happier."

He took a deep breath, feeling his eye well with tears. "I don't know exactly what the rules are or how this works. But, you know...I still need you. So I could say this has been a happy story, or I could *feel* it. We could all feel it. And then we could end this story...together."

He looked up, and light spilled across his face. Then he heard the first beautiful notes of a familiar song: "The Song of the Dead."

Hundreds of paper lamps floated out to sea. Kubo watched as each one lifted into the air and refolded itself, coming together to form a giant paper bird. It was the glowing golden heron, and its light was brighter than ever before.

Kubo smiled, a tear falling down his cheek. His parents were on either side of him. They were there, he knew they were—Hanzo and his mother, their hands on each of his shoulders. For the first time in his life, he didn't need to see them or hear them.... He could *feel* their presence. They were with him, always.

Hundreds of paper lanterns lifted off the river, folding into paper birds to join the rest of the flock. The light danced over Kubo's face. He watched as they circled the sky, darting this way and that in one spectacular display of beauty.

"The end," he whispered, clutching his parents' hands.

And with that, an even more beautiful story began....

DON'T MISS: